W9-AAW-352

I, CROCODILE

FRED MARCELLINO

MICHAEL DI CAPUA BOOKS / HARPER COLLINS PUBLISHERS

TEXT AND PICTURES COPYRIGHT © 1999 BY FRED MARCELLINO / ALL RIGHTS RESERVED / LIBRARY OF CONGRESS CATALOG CARD NUMBER: 99-66181 / FIRST EDITION, 1999
FOR INFORMATION ADDRESS HARPERCOLLINS CHILDREN'S BOOKS, A DIVISION OF HARPERCOLLINS PUBLISHERS, 195 BROADWAY, NEW YORK, NY 10007.
MANUFACTURED IN CHINA.
15 SCP 10 9 8

Ah, what a contented crocodile I used to be. Wallowing around in slimy green water . . . Snoozing on mudbanks in the hot sun . . . Scaring the life out of anything that wandered by.

But my greatest joy? Eating! (Actually, overeating.)

I had the perfect diet. An endless variety of delectable fish, all sorts of succulent water birds, plus a few reptiles on the side—distant cousins only.

However, unlike certain pathetic creatures who have to chase after their next meal, *I* always ate in style.

Dinner? It came to *me*!

And why not? I'm an aristocrat. A direct descendant of the noble crocodiles of ancient Egypt. In fact, the great Pharaohs themselves treated my ancestors like *Gods*!

Idol worship—I just love it! That's why I always resisted eating people, even though they do look awfully tasty. Guess I'm just the sentimental type.

Those were blissful days, indeed. But sadly they came to an abrupt end on (to be precise) August 17, 1799.

Who should decide to come to Egypt?

Napoleon! You know, that French guy who thought he owned the world.

What was going on? An invasion? More like a raid. And in the center of it all, this little man barking orders.

"Mummies! I want mummies!" Napoleon cried. "And a sphinx and an obelisk. Make it a big one! That temple over there? Just what I need! Palm trees, too—don't forget palm trees!"

"And a crocodile," he bellowed. "I must have a crocodile!"

Suddenly some bozos with funny hats and a big net were all over me.

What a cruel and abrupt departure from my mudbank. I scarcely had a chance to give a parting glance to my beloved home, much less finish my scrumptious dessert—
pink flamingo!

And what a beastly ocean voyage. Even crocodiles can get seasick. For the first time in my life, I couldn't eat a thing. I just picked a little.

After two wretched weeks at sea, we finally dropped anchor.

Then an endless coach ride. Was anyone keeping track of all the meals I was missing?

Last stop, Paris!

There, in the gardens, I was installed in a fountain.

How humiliating to find myself living in what amounted to a fancy bathtub.

On the other hand, it *was* rather flattering to receive so much attention.

Napoleon showed me off to everyone.

I was an overnight sensation!

An instant celebrity!

The Toast of the Tuileries!

The Darling of the Empire!

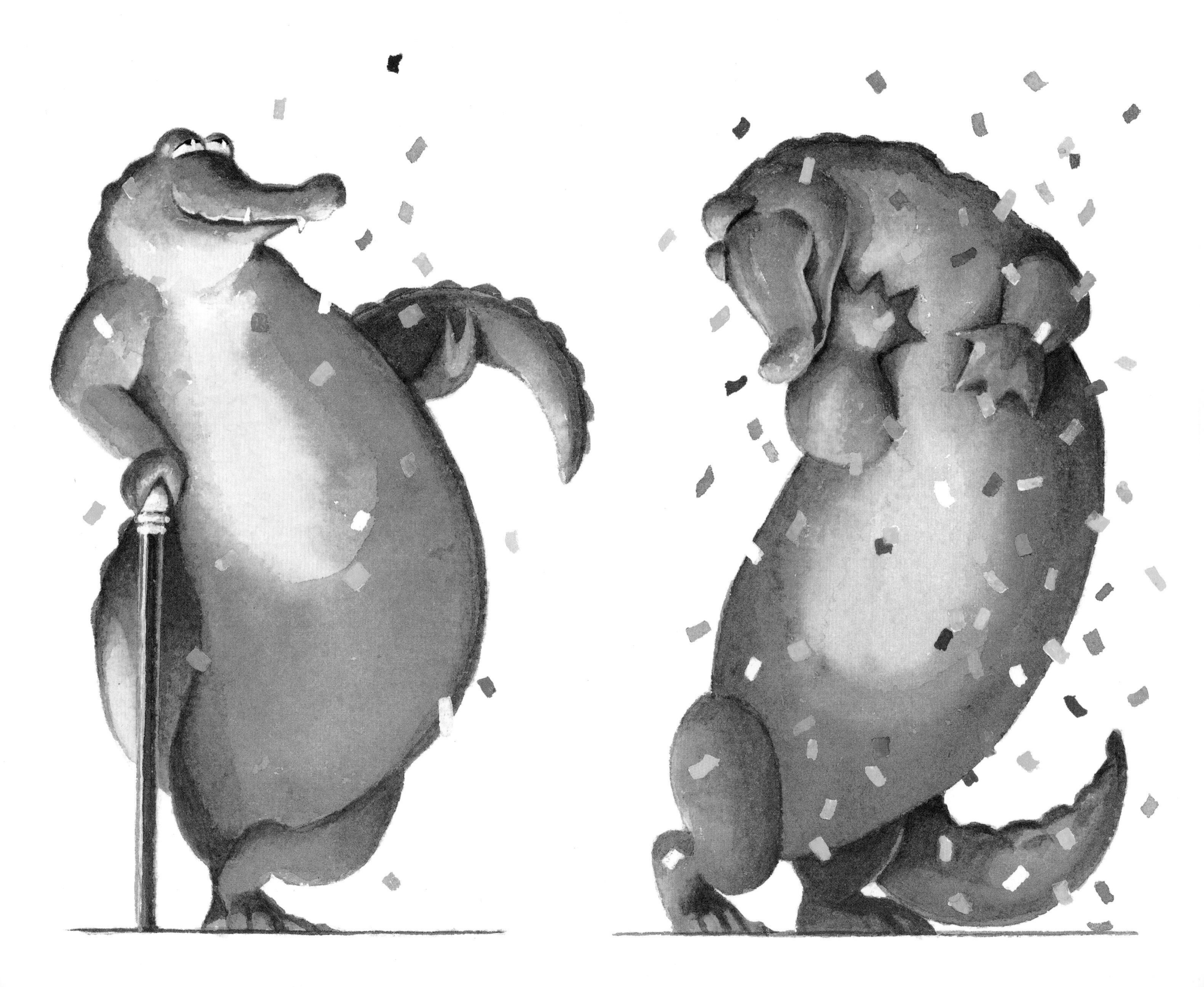

Yes, yes, very nice...
But what about dinner?
I hadn't had a decent meal in ages.

Soon all Paris was doing
The Crocodile Walk.

Well, fashions change quickly in Paris. In no time at all, *Le Fantastique Crocodile Egyptien* was old news.

Napoleon found new amusements.

Visitors were few.

And my diet?

Don't ask.

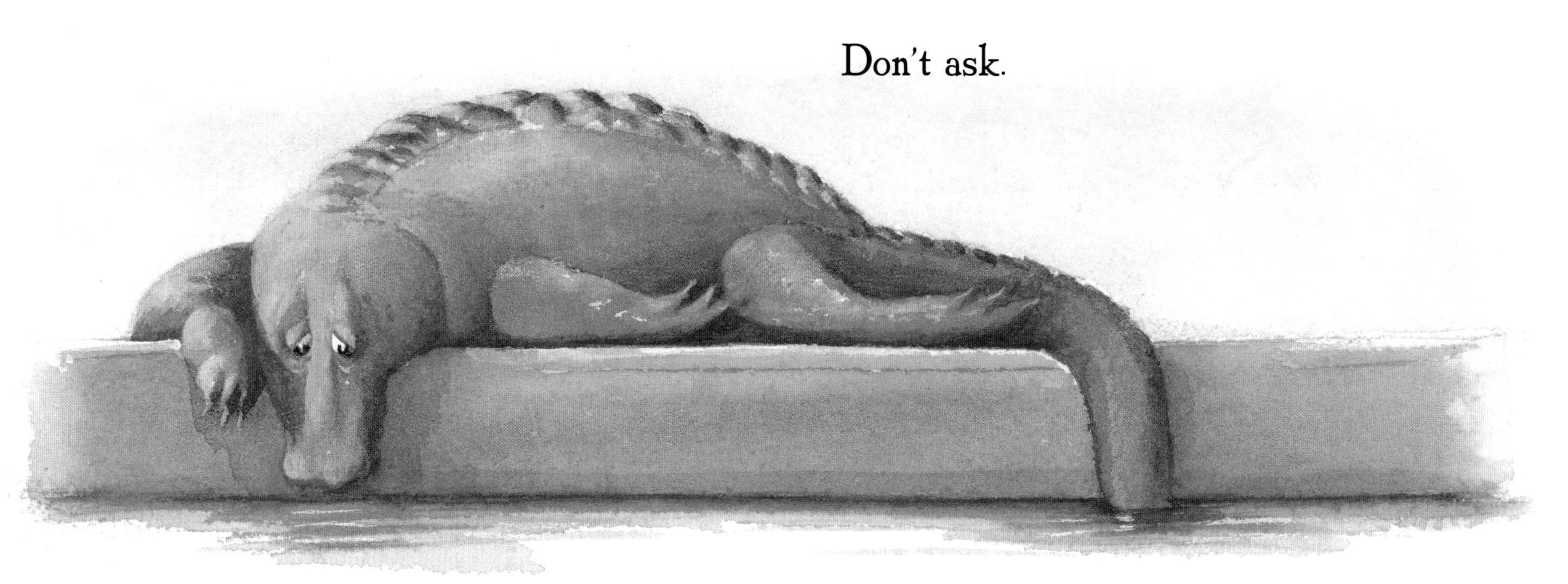

Then one morning Napoleon and some guests strolled idly by.

"Is that beast still here, sir?" inquired one of the ladies. "Off to the kitchen with him! Crocodile pie with Egyptian onions—it's all the rage in Cairo."

"A brilliant idea," cried the Emperor. "We'll have him for dinner tonight."

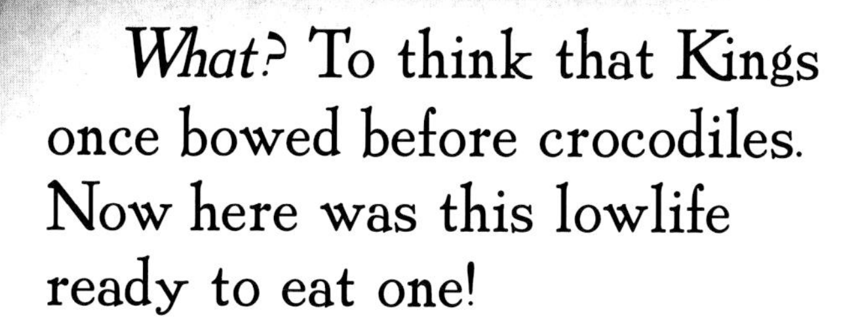

What? To think that Kings once bowed before crocodiles. Now here was this lowlife ready to eat one!

I spent the day nervously pacing the rim of my tub. Then—*oh, no!*—a loutish fellow with a cleaver showed up.

I felt faint.

But wait! A ballooning mishap? Napoleon in peril? My chance to flee!

Boldly seizing the opportunity, I made my escape.

Now what? Murky water, slime-covered walls, dank and fetid air…

Yes! Lucky me. The sewers of Paris!
Crocodile Heaven!

Wait a minute. What about dinner?
Not to mention breakfast,
lunch, and snacks.

After all, I was still stuck in Paris!
What was a starving crocodile supposed to eat?

Yummy! Now what's for dessert?